W9-CNA-112

*Earth's Endangered Creatures*

# PROJECT DOLPHIN

Written by
**Jill Bailey**

*Illustrated by*
**John Green**

STECK-VAUGHN
LIBRARY
A Division of Steck-Vaughn Company

Austin, Texas

*This series is concerned with the world's endangered animals, the reasons why their numbers are diminishing, and the efforts being made to save them from extinction. The author has described these events through the eyes of fictional characters. Although the situations are based on fact, the people and the events described are fictitious.*

Editor: Andy Charman
Designer: Mike Jolley
Picture researcher: Jenny Faithful

**Library of Congress Cataloging-in-Publication Data**

Bailey, Jill.
Project dolphin / written by Jill Bailey;
illustrated by John Green.
p. cm. — (Save our species)
Includes index.
Summary: Linda and her friends observe dolphins in the wild and in captivity. Similar fictional vignettes combined with factual information focus on the behavior and endangered situation of the dolphin.
ISBN 0-8114-2711-0
1. Dolphins—Juvenile fiction. [1. Dolphins—Fiction.]
I. Title. II. Series: Bailey, Jill. Save our species.
PZ10.3.B155Pp          1992          91-16007
[Fic]—dc20                               CIP AC

Color separations by Positive Colour Ltd.,
Maldon, Essex, Great Britain
Printed and bound by L.E.G.O., Vicenza, Italy

1 2 3 4 5 6 7 8 9 0 LE 96 95 94 93 92

# CONTENTS

# DIVING WITH DOLPHINS

**Linda Montgomery** scanned the shimmering sea with her binoculars, hoping to see the dark triangle of a dolphin's fin above the water. Her two friends, Martin Cooper and his young daughter Anita, waited patiently. It was almost an hour before Linda spotted a school of dolphins swimming very near the coast. The three watchers grabbed their binoculars excitedly. They had a good view.

"What kind of dolphins are they?" asked Anita.

"Only common dolphins, I'm afraid," replied Linda. "See how the dorsal fin – the one that sticks up on its back – is dark with a light center. Look too at the

*A bottlenose dolphin shows its teeth. Dolphins feed on fish and squid, which they catch with their sharp, pointed teeth.*

pattern on their flanks, or sides. That paler, yellowish area is shaped like an hourglass."

"There are quite a lot of them," remarked Anita.

"About twenty," said Linda. "That's about the usual size of a school around Ireland. In the Pacific Ocean, there are huge schools of one or two thousand dolphins, all fishing together."

"Do they all belong to one family?" Anita asked.

"Nobody really knows," Linda replied. "It is too difficult to follow a school of wild dolphins all year round to find out. At times they are mainly mothers and calves; other times schools consist of males and females. In very large schools, there are lots of small groups that often break off from the main school. These groups may sleep apart, then come together to feed. This may be because it is easier to see fish with many dolphins looking."

The dolphins were getting closer to shore. Linda was busy writing, noting the pattern of scars and nicks on the fin of each dolphin. She could identify each dolphin by these marks.

*Linda, Martin, and Anita watched the school of dolphins swimming off the rocky Irish coast.*

7

Linda turned to Anita. "Since it's your birthday, how about a special treat?" she asked. "Would you like to swim with a dolphin?"

Anita couldn't believe it!

"What?" she exclaimed. "In the sea? With a real dolphin?"

"Yes," said Linda. "There's a friendly bottlenose dolphin called Paddy who plays with visitors at Ballikenny Bay. Patrick, the fisherman, told me that Paddy was there today."

Soon they were outside Patrick's hut, dragging out his boat and putting on wetsuits.

"Paddy was playing games yesterday," said Patrick. "I was out in the bay trying to bring in my lobster pots, and every time I reached out for the float, he

---

*Most mammals play only when they are young. Adult dolphins enjoy playing as much as any youngster. They have a wonderful sense of humor.*

pushed it farther away. I almost fell in the water the first time."

They scanned the bay for signs of Paddy, and spotted him playing with a rubber dinghy. He was rubbing against it like a cat rubs against a table leg.

The group cruised across the bay in their boat. Soon Paddy was speeding over to them. They slowed the boat down, and Paddy leaped right over it, doing a belly flop that drenched them with water. Martin thought that Paddy had done it on purpose.

*Paddy swam to meet Linda and Anita. Solitary dolphins like Paddy have made friends with divers in many parts of the world.*

As the boat glided to a halt, Linda and Anita slipped quietly into the water. Paddy swam up to Anita immediately. His bright little eyes darted eagerly to and fro. He rolled over. Anita rolled over, too, and soon they were playing a lively game of "copycat." Then, to Anita's dismay, Paddy suddenly swam away.

*Paddy brought Anita a piece of seaweed. Dolphins often start games by offering humans objects from the ocean floor.*

Anita was getting out of the water when Paddy returned. He was carrying a piece of seaweed. Anita reached out for it. Just as she touched it, Paddy dived out of reach. A wild game of tag followed, but Paddy was gentle with Anita. He waited patiently while she came up for air.

As the sun began to set, Linda and Anita reluctantly climbed back into the boat. They heard a cheer from a crowd of people who had gathered on the beach.

"Do dolphins often play with humans?" asked Anita.

"Yes," replied Linda. "Very friendly dolphins like Paddy are rare, though they have been seen in many parts of the world. Ordinarily dolphins don't live alone."

"What were those funny sounds we heard when we were in the water?" asked Anita.

"Those were made by Paddy," said Linda. "Dolphins use sound to find their way underwater, especially deep down or after dark. They send out high-pitched clicks that echo or bounce off any object in their path, such as other fish or boats.

"Dolphins have sharp hearing. They can sort out the different echoes from objects near and far and form a sound picture of their surroundings. They may even detect the contents of other dolphins' stomachs."

*These spinner dolphins, like all dolphins, have smooth, streamlined bodies which allow them to swim with speed.*

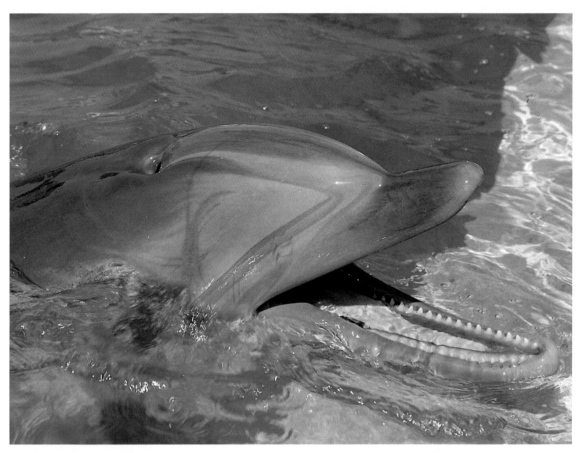

Anita wanted to know more.

"Don't dolphins swallow water when they are calling out to each other?" she asked.

"The sounds don't come from the dolphin's mouth," explained Linda. "They come from its air passages. The dolphin's mouth isn't connected to its lungs. It gets air through the blowhole on the top of its head."

"I didn't see any ears on Paddy," Anita remarked.

"No," agreed Linda. "Their ears are internal. It may be that

*Dolphins take in air through a blowhole on the top of the head. The blowhole closes tightly when a dolphin dives.*

dolphins pick up sound through their chins, which stretch back close to the internal ears."

"Paddy could swim so fast," said Anita, enviously.

"His streamlined shape cuts through the water easily," said Linda. "He has no dangling legs or ears that stick out to push against the water."

"He could dive very deep," said Anita. "Even though he has to come up for air."

"Yes," said Linda. "Some dolphins can go as deep as 2,000 feet. That's because they store oxygen in their blood. They also let their lungs and ribs collapse under the water pressure."

"When we lived on the east coast of England," said Anita, "we found some dolphins stranded on the beach. How do you think they got there?"

"Some scientists think that dolphins use the earth's magnetic field to find their way over long distances," said Linda. "Ear infections or magnetic storms can sometimes upset their magnetic sense. Then they go the wrong way and don't realize it until it is too late."

---

*These dolphins have become stranded on a beach. Once dolphins are out of the water, the weight of their organs presses on their lungs and suffocates them.*

Linda, Martin, and Anita went to a beach cafe for a warm drink. Martin told them about his adventures sailing with Greenpeace. Greenpeace is a conservation organization that is trying to save the dolphins and whales whose numbers are decreasing.

"Our last trip was to the Irish Sea," he said. "We were taking very small samples of their skin and blubber to test them for pollution. Dangerous chemicals such as pesticides collect in the blubber. Some can keep the dolphins from producing young, as well as making them sick."

"Is the Irish Sea very bad?" asked Anita.

"The Irish Sea and the North Sea are badly polluted," said Martin. "The worst place I know of is the St. Lawrence Seaway

---

*The Greenpeace flagship,* Rainbow Warrior, *under sail in the Pacific. Greenpeace campaigns to protect whales and dolphins by drawing public attention to their plight.*

between Canada and the United States. A special group of beluga whales lives there. Belugas are really large, white dolphins. People call them canaries of the sea because they make so many different sounds.

"The number of belugas has been falling rapidly. When the blubber of dead belugas was tested, they found so many pesticides and other dangerous chemicals that the dead bodies were labeled as harmful waste, just like some of the waste from factories. It wasn't safe for humans to get near them.

"The dolphins are also suffering because humans are overfishing the area. When the fish populations fall, so do the numbers of dolphins and porpoises. Worse still, dolphins get blamed for the lack of fish."

---

*For centuries, Arctic peoples have hunted belugas. The bones are used for carving, the skin and blubber are eaten, and the rest of the meat feeds the sled dogs.*

A few months later, Linda was in the warm waters off the coast of Texas. She was taking some tourists to see the spotted dolphins that lived nearby. They were used to visitors.

Several of the females had babies, or calves, with them. Often there was another female helping to care for the calf. These "aunts" stay with the calf while its mother goes to feed. They also bring the calf back to the school if it swims too far.

*A mother dolphin and calf. The calf swims in perfect unison with its mother, keeping just in front of her dorsal fin.*

"How long does the calf stay with its mother?" asked Ben, one of the tourists.

"Up to 18 months," said Linda. "It lives on milk until it's about six months old. Then it begins to fish. Gradually, the milk supply decreases. The calf is ready to breed at age seven."

Some of the tourists got in the water with the dolphins. Linda had fun teaching them to try swimming like dolphins. They had to keep their legs together and beat them up and down. They also had to keep their arms close to their bodies like flippers. Dolphins can swim very fast. Some can reach speeds of over 15 miles an hour.

"If you practice," Linda said, "you will be able to steer by dipping one of your 'flippers.' Now, try not to turn your head. Most dolphins can't turn their necks. That's why they have to swim sideways to see you."

*Dolphins like to follow the waves made by boats. Here they can swim much faster than usual. They seem to like the feel of the frothy water and bubbles.*

The calves returned to their mothers for milk now and then.

"Doesn't the calf get a mouthful of water?" asked Ben.

"No," replied Linda. "The calf presses its tongue against the roof of its mouth and rolls it to form a tube. The mother squirts the milk into this tube. The calf can't take milk, or suck, for long, since it needs to keep going to the surface to breathe. It needs to get its milk as fast as it can."

Suddenly the dolphins were gone. Linda spotted a tall black fin cutting through the water not far away. It was a killer whale, one of the few animals known to attack dolphins. The tourists had seen it too, and were scrambling into the boat.

"It's all right," said Linda. "Killer whales don't usually attack human beings."

"The whale moves a bit like a dolphin," commented Ben.

"Well, it belongs to a family

Above: *A mother dolphin suckling her calf. Dolphin milk contains a lot of fat. On this rich diet, the calf grows quickly.*

Left: *A killer whale approached the tourists and the dolphins. Male killer whales have dorsal fins that can be up to 6 feet high.*

that is more closely related to dolphins than to whales," said Linda. "It feeds like a dolphin, on fish, but also on larger mammals such as sea lions. Killer whales also eat dolphins."

More killer whales appeared.

"Do they hunt in packs?" Ben asked, safely in the boat now.

"Sometimes," said Linda, "and so do dolphins. They will drive fish into shallow water. Then they take turns rushing in to kill them, while the others make sure the fish don't escape."

The whales went on their way, and the tourists headed home.

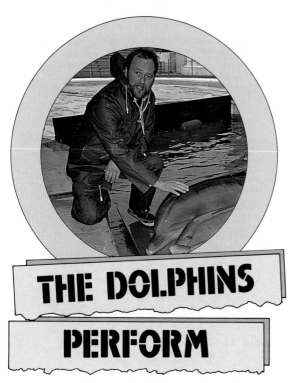

# THE DOLPHINS PERFORM

**Jim Carson** raised his arm and three dolphins leaped out of the water together. They plunged gracefully back into the pool and a shower of spray drenched the onlookers. The afternoon performance at the West Coast Dolphinarium was fun to watch. Linda Montgomery had a pool-side seat. She did not like to see wild animals perform tricks, but she enjoyed the show anyway.

Linda had come to visit Jim to learn more about his research into how dolphins communicate with each other. After the show, she went to talk to him.

"How do you train them to do these things?" she asked.

"They learn quickly," said Jim. "After all, they do many of these things in the wild. Wild dolphins enjoy leaping out of the water for fun, and they are naturally curious about objects they haven't seen before. We give them a reward of fish every time they do the trick right."

"So you don't punish them for not performing or for doing it wrong?" Linda asked.

"No," said Jim, "though dolphinaria in other parts of the world do that. Some put the dolphins in small pens so they

cannot see each other if they perform badly. I don't agree with that kind of punishment."

"Why would they want to take fish as a reward?" asked Linda. "If they are well fed, they shouldn't be interested in fish."

"Well," said Jim, reluctantly, "we feed them a little less when we want to train them."

To Linda's surprise, Jim did not call the dolphins. He simply used hand signals to tell them what he wanted them to do.

---

*Jim had trained his dolphins to perform tricks. Dolphins are very playful animals. Even in the wild, they often leap into the air just for the fun of it.*

Linda watched the three dolphins swimming around their pool. It was a large pool, but it seemed cramped with three dolphins in it. She thought of her wild dolphins, and how they had the whole ocean to play in.

Jim had put on a wetsuit and was with the dolphins in the pool. The big, male dolphin immediately swam up to him and nuzzled him. He was clearly pleased to see Jim. Linda saw Jim playing affectionately with the dolphins. He obviously loved them. He called to her.

"Come in and play," he said. Linda was soon in the pool, too.

*Bottlenose dolphins always look as if they are smiling. In fact, the dolphins' jaws curve upward, so they can't help smiling regardless of how they really feel.*

It seemed oddly quiet to her. When she had dived with wild dolphins, the water had been noisy with clicks and other sounds. Suddenly Linda realized what was missing. There were no rocks, seaweed, or fish. The dolphins had nothing to play with or investigate. There was nothing for them to do except swim around and around.

"There's not much use for

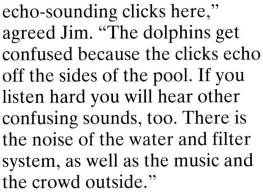

echo-sounding clicks here," agreed Jim. "The dolphins get confused because the clicks echo off the sides of the pool. If you listen hard you will hear other confusing sounds, too. There is the noise of the water and filter system, as well as the music and the crowd outside."

Linda remembered reading how dolphins that are kept in pools suffer from many of the same diseases as humans. The dolphins get diseases caused by stress, such as stomach ulcers and heart attacks. The dolphins couldn't possibly be happy in their small, cramped pool.

*Jim Carson loved to be with his dolphins, and they seemed to enjoy playing with him. Trainers spend a lot of time with their animals, building up their trust.*

"How long do dolphins live in captivity?" Linda asked.

"In some places only about seven or eight years," replied Jim. "They live longer here."

This was just as Linda had feared. Wild dolphins live for at least 40 years. Captive ones need doses of antibiotics and vitamins to keep them alive.

The dolphins were fed only dead fish. Linda had thought that they would at least be allowed to catch live fish.

"That's why they need extra vitamins," said Jim. "Dead fish quickly lose their vitamins."

"Have all these dolphins been caught in the wild?" she asked.

*Jim fed his dolphins with dead fish. Dolphins do not chew the fish; they swallow them whole. Young dolphins have to learn how to turn the fish around to swallow them head first.*

"I'm afraid so," replied Jim. "Dolphins are difficult to breed in captivity. The baby dolphins seldom survive. We think the stress of being in captivity affects their breeding."

"How are wild dolphins caught?" asked Linda.

"In nets," said Jim. "They have to be moved very carefully. Their lungs and hearts are easily crushed by the weight of their bodies once they are out of the water. In the early days, most dolphins died before they got to dolphinaria. Even today more

*A dolphin performing in a show in Florida. Dolphins can propel themselves out of the water with their powerful tails.*

than half of them die. Some die from shock, others from injuries caused by the nets. Sadly, the calves often lose their mothers."

"Aren't there laws against catching dolphins?" she asked.

"Yes," replied Jim. "We have to get licenses to catch them and move them from place to place. Some countries give licenses only to researchers."

Linda wanted to know about Jim's work at the dolphinarium.

"Your dolphins are used for research and entertainment, aren't they?" asked Linda.

"Exactly," said Jim. "Catching dolphins is big business. In the U.S. alone there are over 9,000 jobs in dolphinarium industry. The business is worth about a third of a billion dollars a year. A well-trained dolphin can be worth $80,000; a killer whale, over half a million dollars."

*A school of spinner dolphins off the Leeward Islands, Hawaii. Dolphins travel great distances across the oceans to find food and suitable breeding conditions.*

"I thought the main aim of dolphinaria was to teach people about dolphins," said Linda.

"It is," said Jim. "People can see dolphins for themselves at a dolphinarium. They can see how intelligent, playful, and friendly they are. In this way we can get support and money for saving dolphins in the wild."

Linda thought carefully about what Jim had said. Was it really a good idea for people to see dolphins doing tricks in a pool? She thought that television was a better way of teaching people. A television program could show dolphins and the way they really lived in the wild, enjoying the freedom of the open oceans.

"Can I see what you are doing in your research?" Linda asked.

"Come down to the pool after breakfast tomorrow, and I'll show you," promised Jim.

Linda arrived at the pool early the following morning. Jim was attaching small light bulbs onto the dolphins' heads. There were five dolphins in the pool.

"I'm trying to find out how they talk to each other," he said.

*The dolphins seem to enjoy their performances. After the show, Linda noticed that the dolphins seemed bored in their small pool.*

Jim began to explain his work. "Each dolphin has its own unique whistle," he said. "It is different from the clicking it uses for echolocation. When one dolphin meets another, it calls out with its whistle. The sound seems to say, 'This is me.' We have a new dolphin arriving in half an hour. I want to see how the others greet it."

"Why are you using light bulbs?" asked Linda.

"They don't use their mouths to whistle," said Jim, "so it's hard to tell which one is calling.

*Dolphins' calls come from deep inside their air passages, not from their throats. A large pad of fatty tissue in their foreheads, the melon, produces the sounds.*

These different-colored bulbs light up when the dolphin calls, so I can see who is whistling."

Jim lowered a hydrophone, a special microphone, into the water. It would pick up the dolphins' calls and record them as a series of zigzags on a roll of paper. Jim would then have a record of all that happened.

"You trained dolphins for the Navy, didn't you?" asked Linda.

"Yes," replied Jim. "Dolphins' echolocation is ten times more efficient than Navy radar. The Navy wants to find out more about how the dolphins do it."

"The Navy uses dolphins, doesn't it," asked Linda.

"Yes," said Jim. "Dolphins can be trained to lay mines, or to recover equipment that has been lost at sea."

*Jim lowered a hydrophone into the pool. This waterproof instrument picks up the sounds made by the dolphins. These can be recorded on paper or tape.*

Linda shuddered.

"If the Navy uses them in that way," she said, "any nation at war with the U.S. might start killing every dolphin it found."

They were interrupted by the arrival of the new dolphin. The other dolphins greeted it. The first to approach was the large male dolphin, but the females soon followed. The hydrophone recorded all the sounds that they made.

"Do they have real conversations?" asked Linda.

"We don't think so," replied Jim. "They don't make enough different kinds and patterns of sounds to have a language. They do, however, recognize single signs and signs combined to make a kind of language. I've been teaching them hand signals. I'll show you."

Linda was amazed. By using hand signals, Jim could make the dolphins pick up balls or a rubber ring, and perform tricks with them. They knew the signs for "diving," "fetching," and "tossing in the air" and "high," "low," "right," and "left."

"How intelligent do you think dolphins are?" asked Linda.

"That's a tough one," said Jim. "Their brains are large, but scientists believe that may be because they don't dream when they sleep. They think dreaming is one way for the brain to get rid of unwanted information, to allow new information to come in. Dolphins do not dream, so they need larger brains to store all the extra information."

Left: *The hydrophone's recording showed that the new dolphin often copied the other dolphins' calls, as if to answer.*

Above: *Dolphins in an aquarium. They can be trained to do many tricks, but it is unfair to test their intelligence on human terms.*

*In cold waters, dolphins are kept warm by a layer of fat, or blubber, just beneath the skin.*

A few weeks later Linda and Jim watched a rare moment. One of the dolphins gave birth. The mother and another female had moved away from the other dolphins in the pool. The calf's tail gradually appeared, and very slowly the rest of it slid out. The second female nudged the calf and placed herself just beneath it. Then, she lifted the calf gently to the surface of the water so that it could take its first breath. Soon it was swimming close to its mother.

"I thought that baby mammals were usually born head first," remarked Linda.

"Most species are," said Jim, "but they are not born at sea. Like all baby mammals, baby dolphins have lungs and need to breathe. If they were born head first they might drown before the rest of the body emerged, so they usually come out tail first."

Linda was surprised that the calf was already quite large.

"Oceans are cold places in which to live," Jim explained. "Large animals keep warm more easily than small ones."

"Do dolphins bear young in pools as often as in the open ocean?" asked Linda.

"Yes," said Jim, "there's little difference."

"So dolphins produce only one calf about every two years," said Linda.

"It's usually longer than that," said Jim. "That's one reason to worry about their falling numbers. It is hard for dolphin populations to grow once they have been overhunted."

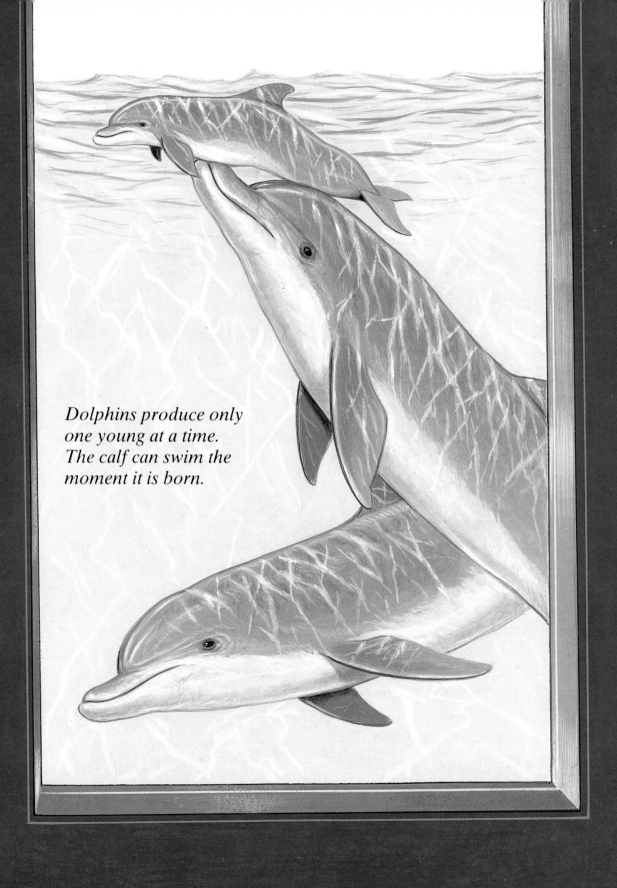

Dolphins produce only
one young at a time.
The calf can swim the
moment it is born.

# THE TUNA CATCH

**Ken Barnes** scanned the glistening water of the Pacific with his binoculars. He was a member of a tuna boat crew and was searching for dolphins. In the eastern Pacific, yellowfin tuna gather in large schools beneath traveling schools of dolphins. If Ken could find dolphins, he would find tuna.

High above Ken, in the look-out post, his friend Gordon Griffin was also looking for dolphins. Suddenly Gordon shouted. There, in the distance, were the outlines of dolphins swimming across the water.

As the boat sped toward the dolphins, the crew sprang into action. They launched a speedboat to stop the dolphins. It would drop small bombs to frighten and confuse them. At the same time, the huge, almost circular net was slowly let out. The net was also guided by men in speedboats, who encircled the dolphins and drove them into the middle of the net.

The dolphins were confused. They leaped into the air and collided with each other in an effort to escape. As the net closed in, the dolphins' panic grew. Their shrieks could be heard even from the boat. Some were unable to come up for air, and were drowning.

*The huge tuna nets can stretch for nearly half a mile. Large loans of money are needed to buy such equipment. This means that the boats need to make huge catches to repay the money to the banks.*

*A school of spinner dolphins. For some unknown reason, yellowfin tuna collect in large numbers beneath dolphin schools.*

Ken was unaware of the full horror of what was happening as he prepared to land the tuna catch. To him, dolphins were just big fish that attracted tuna, but got in the way of the nets.

The boat reversed slowly, and the net changed shape, allowing some dolphins to escape. The United States has laws that limit the number of dolphins that can be killed by tuna fishermen. When a strong wind began to blow, the captain ordered the boat to stop. It would have been dangerous to go on.

More and more dolphins were getting tangled in the net as it

*A Greenpeace diver releasing a Pacific white-sided dolphin from a net. Over 120,000 dolphins are killed every year by tuna nets.*

was hauled on deck by a huge motor-powered winch.

When the catch was on board, the men moved in to separate the dying and dead dolphins from the fish.

"Another disastrous catch," said Ken to Gordon.

"Yes," replied Gordon. "It's good we don't have an official observer with us. In the old days, they used poles and lines instead of nets. They'd throw bait into the water and start a feeding frenzy. The tuna didn't even notice if there was bait on a hook or not. Dolphins are smarter; they avoided hooks."

*Ben Deeble of Greenpeace with a dolphin killed in a drift net in the Tasman Sea, near Australia. Thousands of dolphins are killed in fishermen's nets every year.*

"Speaking of fishing lines," said Ken, "why don't we take the motorboat and go fishing after this catch is over?"

The following evening, Ken and Gordon set off in the small motorboat. Suddenly, they were no longer alone. A large school of spinner dolphins began following the boat. The dolphins leaped high into the air and spun around and around before dropping back into the water in a spray of sparkling droplets. Ken leaned over the boat to watch them. Suddenly, his cap fell into the water, and was soon far behind them. Gordon turned the boat around. They found the cap. A group of dolphins was playing with it. Ken watched them, entranced, then thought of the previous evening's catch. He felt guilty when he thought of the dying dolphins.

Gordon tried to make him feel better about the dolphins.

"We're not the only culprits," he said. "The drift nets they set all over the world kill thousands of dolphins. Some nets are up to 50 miles long, and trap anything that happens to swim into them. Dolphins, turtles, seals, and sea-birds are all caught in those nets. We're not deliberately hunting the dolphins, like they do in some parts of the world."

"Well," said Ken, "there's too much money tied up in these boats and nets to go back to the old ways now."

Below: *A group of spinner dolphins swam to meet Gordon and Ken. Spinner dolphins can leap into the air and spin three or four times before falling into the water.*

Above: *A white-tipped shark caught in a drift net in the Tasman Sea. Drift nets stretch for up to 50 miles through the world's oceans, forming walls of death.*

Ken Barnes was on leave. His young son, Dan, had persuaded Ken to take him to a small bay, where he had heard there was a friendly wild dolphin.

When they arrived at the bay, they found some people leaning over the seawall. There were two swimmers in the water. Dan and Ken saw a dolphin frolicking with them. One of the swimmers turned and saw Dan. It was his old scoutmaster.

"Come on in, Dan," he called.

Dan was soon in among them. To his delight the dolphin came

*Dolphins are social animals. They live in schools containing individuals of both sexes and all ages. Solitary dolphins are rare.*

up and nuzzled him gently. Gradually Dan and the dolphin drifted away from the others. Ken watched anxiously. Then the dolphin left Dan to see what the other swimmers were doing.

Suddenly, Dan was shouting "help." He had a cramp. He was waving his arms as he sank.

The other swimmers swam toward him, but the dolphin got

there first. The dolphin placed itself under Dan, and lifted him to the surface. The dolphin then swam slowly toward the shore with Dan lying across its back. Ken couldn't believe his eyes. The dolphin had probably saved Dan's life.

When Dan was safe and warm, the others joined them for a hot drink.

"We're going to watch some films about dolphins tonight," said the scoutmaster. "It will be interesting. Why not join us?"

---

*The dolphin carried Dan back to the shore. Many instances in which drowning humans have been rescued by dolphins have been recorded. Dolphins seem to be especially fond of children.*

The first film showed how a school of dolphins lived. The audience saw them hunt and play, and saw how females help to look after each other's young. They saw how dolphins help each other when they are hurt, even if it means they will be hurt, too. Dolphins will return to help an injured dolphin escape from hunters, or to lift it gently to the surface to breathe.

Ken began to feel discomfort.

---

*Ken and Dan visited the bay once more. The dolphin was still there. Ken knew that he could not return to the tuna boat.*

Next, to his horror, was a film about tuna fishing. He'd never told Dan exactly how he caught tuna. Now he was seeing it in detail. Dan stared at his father in disbelief.

"Do you really do that?" he asked, afraid of the answer.

"Yes," muttered Ken.

"How could you?" Dan asked.

"I didn't know dolphins were so intelligent and good to each other," said Ken.

"I'm never going to eat yellowfin tuna again," Dan asserted. "You can't go back on the boat, Dad. Not after this."

"No," said Ken. He knew he would not be able to face Dan again if he did.

"What can you do instead?" asked Dan.

"I don't know," said Ken. "In other parts of the Pacific, they catch other kinds of tuna with no harm to dolphins. Perhaps I could get a job with them. The pay isn't as good, though. Or I might set up my own business. We could catch yellowfin tuna the old way, with lines and hooks. The problem is that tuna caught the old way is more expensive to buy and not all stores will stock it. I'll talk to my friend Gordon about it."

Later, Ken and Dan visited the bay. In the distance a sleek, dark shape swam in the water. The dolphin was still there.

*Dolphins can teach us a lot. Most importantly, we must learn how to live in peace with the creatures who share our planet.*

# DOLPHIN
# UPDATE

There are many species of dolphins. It is difficult to say which ones are true dolphins. Some species called porpoises in the U.S. are called dolphins elsewhere and some species called whales are closer to dolphins than to whales.

True dolphins are those belonging to the *Delphinidae* family. True porpoises belong to the family *Phocoenidae*. River dolphins, which live in fresh water, belong to four different families.

## THREATS TO DOLPHINS
Dolphin populations all over the world are declining rapidly.

• The biggest threat comes from drift nets in most of the world's oceans. These nets kill many different species. The nets of eastern Pacific yellowfin tuna boats kill mainly spotted and spinner dolphins.
• In some parts of the oceans, dolphins are hunted for food, fertilizer, or fishing bait.
• In some parts of the world, the fishing industry has taken so many fish from the sea that food for dolphins is scarce.
• Dolphins all over the world are at risk from pollution. River dolphins suffer most from this.

**Long-finned Pilot Whale**

**Killer Whale**

**Killer Whale** • Killer whales belong to the dolphin family. They are found in all oceans. The male may be up to 23 feet long. It is a powerful animal with a broad head and distinctive black and white markings. Its flippers are rounded and the female's dorsal fin is curved; the male's is straight and tall .

**Pilot Whale** • Pilot whales are dolphins. There are two species. The long-finned pilot whale is found all over the world, but the short-finned type lives mainly in tropical and subtropical waters. Males grow up to 18 feet long. Pilot whales have a square, bulbous head, and a patch of gray on the chin.

**Common or Saddleback Dolphin** • This species is found in all tropical, subtropical and warm temperate oceans, and also in the Mediterranean and Black seas. Male common dolphins reach a length of about 7 feet. This species has a slender body, a slender snout, a slender central dorsal fin, and an hourglass pattern of yellow or tan on its flanks.

**Common Dolphin**

**Bottlenose Dolphin** • Bottlenose dolphins are found in the coastal waters of most tropical, subtropical, and temperate oceans and seas. Males can be up to 13 feet long. This species has a large head and short beak, often with a pale patch near the tip of the lower jaw. The dorsal fin is tall, slender, and curved.

**Bottlenose Dolphin**

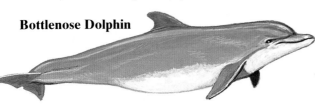

**River Dolphin** • Chinese river dolphins spend their entire lives in fresh water. They live in mostly muddy rivers where they rely on echolocation to find their way and hunt.

**River Dolphin**

**Spinner Dolphin** • This species is found in most tropical waters. Male spinner dolphins are up to 6 feet long. There is a distinct black or gray stripe from the flipper to the eye, and a slender central dorsal fin which is often paler in the middle. This species is slim with a slim beak. It is named for its ability to leap into the air and spin before dropping back into the sea.

**Spinner Dolphin**

**Spotted Dolphin** • This species is found in the tropical Atlantic Ocean. Male spotted dolphins reach a length of 7 feet. This is a sturdy species with distinctive markings, and a curved centrally-placed dorsal fin. The long slender beak has pale gray or white lips.

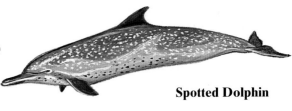

**Spotted Dolphin**

**Narwhal** • Narwhals come from the family *Monodontidae* which includes the belugas, and are very like dolphins. The male narwhal has a single, large spiral tusk up to 9 feet long sticking out from its upper jaw. Nobody knows what it is for, but it seems to be used in mock fights between rival males.

**Narwhal**

# INDEX

## Useful Address

If you are interested in dolphins, you may want to write to the following organization for information about the campaign to save and protect these marine animals.

Save the Dolphins Project
Earth Island Institute
300 Broadway, #28
San Francisco, CA 94133

## Picture credits
(*a*=above, *m*=middle, *b*=below)
Cover: *Portraits: a* Philip Hargraves; *m* Planet Earth Pictures; *b* Philip Hargraves
*Dolphin:* Jeff Foott/Bruce Coleman Ltd.

*Page 5* Bruce Coleman Ltd; *page 6* George Bingham/Bruce Coleman Ltd; *page 8* John Cancalosi/Bruce Coleman Ltd; *page 11* L.C. Marigo/Bruce Coleman Ltd; *page 12* R. Van Nostrand/Frank Lane Picture Agency; *page 14* Grace/Greenpeace; *page 15* Norman Tomalin/Bruce Coleman Ltd; *page 16* Frank Lane Picture Agency; *page 19* Jeff Foott/Bruce Coleman Ltd; *page 22* Stephen J. Krasemann/Bruce Coleman Ltd; *page 25* Jeff Foott/Bruce Coleman Ltd; *page 26* Frans Lanting/Bruce Coleman Ltd; *page 28* Hans Reinhard/Bruce Coleman Ltd; *page 35* L.C. Marigo/Bruce Coleman Ltd; *pages 36, 37 and 39* Grace/Greenpeace; *page 40* Frank Lane Picture Agency; *page 43* Christian Zuber/Bruce Coleman Ltd.

## A Templar Book
Devised and produced by The Templar Company plc
Pippbrook Mill, London Road, Dorking
Surrey RH4 1JE, Great Britain